For my favorite little big girls: Lilly, Grace,
Fiona, Adele, Marianne, and Annabel
—A. P.

To my mom, Anne, who taught me to see adventure wherever I go
—M. M.

For Shaun, my big brother living in the Big Apple
—K. V.

SIMON & SCHUSTER BOOKS FOR YOUNG READERS
An imprint of Simon & Schuster Children's Publishing Division
1230 Avenue of the Americas, New York, New York 10020
Text copyright © 2019 by Allison Pataki and Marya Myers
Illustrations copyright © 2019 by Kristi Valiant
SIMON & SCHUSTER BOOKS FOR YOUNG READERS is a trademark of Simon & Schuster, Inc.
For information about special discounts for bulk purchases,
please contact Simon & Schuster Special Sales at 1-866-506-1949 or business@simonandschuster.com.
The Simon & Schuster Speakers Bureau can bring authors to your live event.
For more information or to book an event, contact the Simon & Schuster Speakers Bureau
at 1-866-248-3049 or visit our website at www.simonspeakers.com.
Book design by Laurent Linn
The text for this book was set in Minister Std.
The illustrations for this book were created using a mix of the illustrator's photos and painting digitally in Photoshop.
Manufactured in China
0219 SCP
First Edition
2 4 6 8 10 9 7 5 3 1
Library of Congress Cataloging-in-Publication Data
Names: Pataki, Allison, author. | Myers, Marya, author. | Valiant, Kristi, illustrator.
Title: Nelly takes New York : a little girl's adventures in the Big Apple / Allison Pataki, Marya Myers ; illustrated by Kristi Valiant.
Description: First edition. | New York : Simon & Schuster Books for Young Readers, [2019] | Series: Big city adventures |
Summary: Nelly and her beagle Bagel set out on a tour of their home, New York City, in search of the "Big Apple."
Identifiers: LCCN 2017060006 (print) | LCCN 2018004093 (eBook) |
ISBN 9781534425040 (hardcover : alk. paper) | ISBN 9781534425057 (eBook)
Subjects: LCSH: New York (N.Y.)—Juvenile fiction. | CYAC: New York (N.Y.)—Fiction. |
Beagle (Dog breed)—Fiction. | Dogs—Fiction.
Classification: LCC PZ7.1.P376 (eBook) | LCC PZ7.1.P376 Nel 2019 (print) | DDC [E]—dc23
LC record available at https://lccn.loc.gov/2017060006

NELLY TAKES
NEW YORK

A Little Girl's Adventures in the Big Apple

BY **Allison Pataki** AND **Marya Myers**

ILLUSTRATED BY **Kristi Valiant**

SIMON & SCHUSTER BOOKS FOR YOUNG READERS

New York   London   Toronto   Sydney   New Delhi

Nelly wakes to all the sounds of her home—
New York City.

The subway rumbles.

A musician *rat-tat-tats* his drum.

The gate to the flower store rattles as
Mr. Lee opens for business.

Nelly nudges her beagle, Bagel, awake.

"We can't sleep away such a beautiful day."

On the corner of her sunny **West Village** street,
Mr. Patel sells coffee and breakfast from his cart.
"Good morning, Nelly! The usual?"
"Not today, Mr. Patel. We're headed to the
farmers market at **Union Square**."
"Sounds great! The Big Apple is tons of fun!"

"A Big Apple?" Nelly says. "Bagel,
are you thinking what I'm thinking?"
"Ruff!" says Bagel.
"We have to find it!"
"Ruff!" Bagel agrees.

Nelly and Bagel reach the bustling market. They sample delicious breads, colorful jams, and fresh-squeezed juices. Nelly looks through the crowd and spots a huge basket.

"That must be it!"

She runs to the table and peeks inside, and
finds ripe, red—but they are all the same size!
"Where is the *Big* Apple?" Nelly asks.

The farmer laughs. "If you really want
to see the Big Apple, you should go to the
natural history museum!"

"A museum?" Nelly says. "The apple must be so big that it needs to be studied!"

She scoops up Bagel and runs off toward the subway.

The enormous columns in front of the **American Museum of Natural History** almost reach the clouds! Nelly and Bagel hurry inside, afraid the Big Apple will be cut up for science before they have a chance to see it!

They race through a
maze of students and
tourists and artifacts.

"Found it!"
Nelly exclaims.

"Bagel, no!" Nelly says, but Bagel
wiggles free and races toward the curtain.

Just then the curator begins: "I would like to introduce the latest addition to our collection. . . ."

The curator prepares to pull down the curtain, but Bagel beats him to it.

"A triceratops!" the curator bellows. Luckily, Bagel ducks out of sight just as everyone's eyes are drawn up toward the skeleton of the beast.

Nelly is confused. "A dinosaur! But where is the Big Apple?"

A fellow museum visitor hears the question. "If you really want to see the Big Apple, you should head to the heart of New York City: **Central Park**!"

"Central Park?" Nelly repeats. "I bet the apple is so big it can't fit indoors!"

Just then the boy with him says, "I thought a triceratops had three horns?"

"Bagel!" says Nelly, and she tucks
him under her arm and hurries outside.

In Central Park, they find a big zoo. What a sight! Families from all over gather to see the exotic animals. But Nelly is busy following the flash of red above everyone's heads.

"That must be it, Bagel!"
Nelly points.

When they finally push to the front, they see only sea lions playing catch. The happy audience roars with approval and the sea lions bow their heads. Nelly and Bagel join in the clapping then head deeper into the park.

"This place is huge!" Nelly exclaims.

They decide to pick up some ice cream and rest at a pond.

"How will we ever find the Big Apple?" Nelly asks.

A family of French tourists overhears Nelly. The mother says,
"We love to visit New York City! But when we want to feel what
the Big Apple is truly about, we go to the **9/11 Memorial**."
"*Merci!*" Nelly replies, and races off to catch the subway.

Downtown, the crowds gather around two large, peaceful pools. People walk around, holding the hands of their loved ones.

"This must be the place," Nelly remarks. "A spot this special has to hold the Big Apple. Right, Bagel? Bagel!"

"Oh no!" she cries out, looking around for her dog. How will she ever find him among all these people?

"Can I help you, miss?" a police officer asks.

"I can't find my dog anywhere," Nelly cries.
"Don't worry, we will help you look for him."

Just then someone rolls up on a bicycle, and there, sitting in the front basket, is Bagel! "Does this little guy belong to you?" the biker asks. "I found him scuffling with some pigeons over at the pretzel cart."

"Bagel!" Nelly shouts, hugging her dog and thanking the friendly New Yorkers who have helped.

Nelly sits down with Bagel and sighs. "Oh, Bagel, I'm glad that I found you. But I don't think we'll ever find the Big Apple."

Just then, the door to a yellow taxi opens. The driver gets out and calls, "Don't give up, miss! I drive all over this city day and night. There is only one place in this city to truly see the whole Big Apple. Hop in!"

The taxi jerks to a stop in front of a very tall building on the
corner of Fifth Avenue and Thirty-Fourth Street. Nelly reads
the giant gold letters that say **Empire State Building**.

The sun is beginning to go down as the elevator goes up. Nelly and Bagel count every floor they pass, wondering how they will be able to see the Big Apple from the top of such a tall building.

The elevator chimes at floor 102. The doors open and . . .

The lights of New York City from the **Freedom Tower at the World Trade Center** to the **Cathedral of Saint John the Divine** by Columbia University are glowing and dancing in Nelly's eyes.

A tour guide says to a group, "The Empire State Building is the third tallest building in New York City. It was once the tallest building in the world! With views on all sides, you can see it all: the **Big Apple—New York City**. Eat it up, ladies and gentlemen!"

As the sun sets over the Hudson River and the lights of the city begin to glow brighter, Nelly thinks about everyone she's met today. Some of those people call New York City home. Some of them are tourists from all over the world. All of them have come to experience the unique city.

Each one of them has helped her to get to this spot.

"That's it, Bagel!" Nelly exclaims. "The Big Apple isn't something you can hold or eat. The Big Apple is all of us— **the Big Apple IS New York City!**"

When Nelly and Bagel make their way back toward home,
Mr. Patel is there to toss Nelly a big juicy apple.
Nelly takes a big bite.
Crunch!